WALTZ OF THE SNOWFLAKES

ELLY MACKAY

RP|KIDS
PHILADELPHIA

To Simon, always.

Running Press Kids
Hachette Book Group
1290 Avenue of the Americas, New York, NY 10104
www.runningpress.com/rpkids
@RP_Kids

Printed in China

First Edition: October 2017

Published by Running Press Kids, an imprint of Perseus Books, LLC,
a subsidiary of Hachette Book Group, Inc.

The Hachette Speakers Bureau provides a wide range of authors for speaking events.
To find out more, go to www.hachettespeakersbureau.com or call (866) 376-6591.

The publisher is not responsible for websites (or their content) that are not owned by the publisher.

Print book cover and interior design by Frances J. Soo Ping Chow

Library of Congress Control Number: 2016953721

ISBNs: 978-0-7624-5338-2 (hardcover); 978-0-7624-6227-8 (ebook);
978-0-7624-6427-2 (ebook); 978-0-7624-6428-9 (ebook)

1010

11 10 9 8 7 6 5 4 3 2

ACT ONE

INTERMISSION

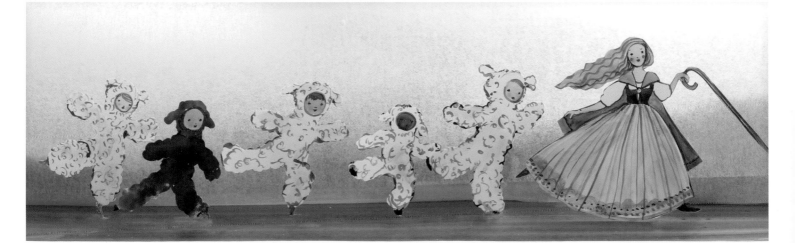